AXEL STORM

PIRATE CURSE

For Jeff "Pirate Jeff" Pleadwell

ORCHARD BOOKS
338 Euston Road, London NW1 3BH
Orchard Books Australia
Level 17/207 Kent Street, Sydney, NSW 2000

First published in 2010
First paperback publication in 2011

ISBN 978 1 40830 263 7 (hardback)
ISBN 978 1 40830 271 2 (paperback)

Text and illustrations © Shoo Rayner 2010

The right of Shoo Rayner to be identified as the author and
illustrator of this work has been asserted by him in accordance
with the Copyright, Designs and Patents Act, 1988.

A CIP catalogue record for this book is available
from the British Library.

1 3 5 7 9 10 8 6 4 2 (hardback)
1 3 5 7 9 10 8 6 4 2 (paperback)

Printed in Great Britain

Orchard Books is a division of Hachette Children's Books,
an Hachette UK company.

PIRATE CURSE

SHOO RAYNER

ORCHARD BOOKS

CHAPTER ONE

"*Dubbly! Dubbly! Dubbly!*"

Axel Storm leapt off his chair. "What is that noise? It's been going on for ages!"

"I – think – it's – out – side." Dad was distracted. He was playing *Pirate Curse* on the computer and trying to beat Axel's best ever score.

"You're not cheating enough, Dad!"
Axel sighed. "You'll never win *Pirate
Curse* if you don't cheat."

"*Dubbly! Dubbly! Dubbly!*"

"What *is* that?" Axel thought he was
going mad. He decided to investigate.

Enormous glass doors swished open, letting him out onto the beach terrace. The fabulous turquoise sea lay just beyond a line of palm trees. Waves gently lapped the dazzling, golden sandy shore.

This was Mum and Dad's holiday island. They owned it all.

Axel's mum and dad were rock stars. Their band, Stormy Skies, had recorded twenty-two platinum-selling hits in eighty-three different countries around the world. They spent half their lives travelling, performing concerts and meeting their millions of fans.

The Storms were rich – really, really rich. But even though they were richer than you can ever imagine being rich, they still tried to live normal lives.

They only had four cooks…

…three maids…

…ten gardeners…

…a swimming pool in the shape of a
pineapple…

…and a games room with all the latest
games consoles.

Their giant mansion house was built
into the hillside. It looked like a villain's
lair in an old spy movie. Axel liked to
imagine that there was a space rocket
launch bay hidden inside the hill!

But it wasn't always fun to be the son of famous parents.

Gazing at the beautiful ocean, all Axel wanted to do was jump in and swim around with his scuba-diving equipment to see the amazing fish and corals on the reef.

But he wasn't allowed to, because not far away a photographers' boat bobbed gently on the waves. Wherever the Storm family went, press photographers followed them – even on their summer holidays!

"That horrid Archie Flash from *Celebrity Gossip Magazine* is just waiting to get a picture of you," his mother had explained. "We want you to be able to grow up like any other normal child."

Just then, Axel heard the noise again.

"*Dubbly! Dubbly! Dubbly!*"

"What the…"

A bright-green parrot shot past Axel and swooped into the games room.

"*Dubbly! Dubbly! Dubbly!*"

"Yikes!" Dad threw his games controller into the air and cowered behind the sofa. "Get that thing out of here!" he whimpered.

The parrot landed on their computer keyboard and tapped on the keys.

"*Dubbly! Dubbly! Dubbly!*"

As the parrot spoke, the letters "www" appeared on the high intensity, laser-vision projection wall.

"It's logging onto a website!" Axel gasped.

The parrot typed in a password and a familiar face appeared on the screen.

"*Arrrr*. Be that you, Thrust?"

A raspy, pirate sort of voice boomed out of the digital surround-sound speakers.

Dad peeped out from his hiding place. "It's Uncle Rackham!" he cheered.

Uncle Rackham wore a red bandanna on his head and a gold earring in his right ear. He looked like a pirate!

"I sent Caw Caw over to see if you were at home," Uncle Rackham explained.

Axel and his dad looked at each other. "Who's Caw Caw?"

The parrot spread her wings wide and shrieked, "Caw! Caw!"

"Can I borrow Axel for a few days?" Uncle Rackham asked. "I need help. I'm…" He hushed his voice and whispered, "I'm searching for pirate treasure!"

"Pirate treasure!" Axel whooped. "Please let me go, Dad!"

"Your mum would never agree," Dad said, trying to think of a reason to say no.

"But I'm *so-o-o-o-o* bored here," Axel wailed.

It was true. There was nothing for Axel to do on the island without being photographed for the papers.

"Oh…all right, then," Dad said reluctantly. "You can go, but Uncle Rackham will have to smuggle you off the island without anyone noticing. And I don't want you having one of your wild adventures!"

"Yee-hah!" Axel whooped.

"Who's a lucky boy, then!" shrieked Caw Caw.

CHAPTER TWO

Next morning, Uncle Rackham stormed
up the beach with an enormous canvas
kitbag thrown over his shoulder.

"Axel, me lad!" he boomed, ruffling
Axel's hair. "Haven't you grown?"

Axel smiled politely. Why did
grown-ups always say that?

Dad and Uncle Rackham hugged and playfully punched each other on the arm.

"How are you going to get Axel off the island without *them* seeing?" Mum asked, pointing at the photographers' boat. The sun reflected off their long-range camera lenses.

"Har-har!" Uncle Rackham tapped his nose and patted the kitbag. "I'll stick 'im in 'ere!" he laughed.

The kitbag had been stuffed with old palm leaves to make it look full. When it was empty, Axel wriggled inside. Uncle Rackham lifted him onto his shoulder and plonked him in the hull of his boat, along with the scuba-diving equipment which Axel was taking with him.

"Be careful," said Mum. "Make sure Axel wears a hat and puts on lots of sun cream. Do feed him properly…and don't let him have *any* adventures!" she said firmly.

"Who's a good boy?" Caw Caw screeched.

It was hot and airless in the kitbag. The rocking boat made Axel feel seasick. It was a wonderful relief to breathe fresh air when Uncle Rackham let him out of the bag.

"It's safe now, Axel," he said. "We're way out of sight of prying cameras."

Axel stood up and stretched. It was good to feel the sun and the salty sea spray on his face. It was the first time he had felt free since the holidays began.

The tiny boat had outriggers on each side that helped it skim across the waves. Axel could feel the ocean slipping beneath the hull. The triangular sail flapped and strained as the wind blew them towards Uncle Rackham's island.

Caw Caw sat on top of the mast and made helpful suggestions. "Splice the mainbrace! Keelhaul the landlubbers!"

"How do you know which way to go?" Axel asked. "Have you got satellite navigation?"

Uncle Rackham threw back his head and roared with laughter. "You don't need all that stuff!"

He passed something to Axel. It was a collection of sticks and seashells, tied together in a strange, random pattern.

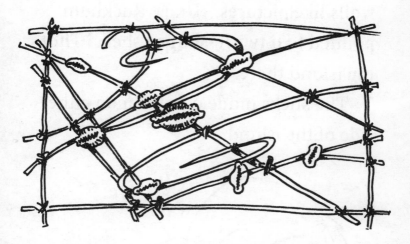

"It's a stick map," Uncle Rackham explained. "The sticks represent the direction of tides and currents. The shells are the islands. Once you learn how to read the map, you can sail anywhere you like. They've been used for thousands of years."

Axel studied the fragile object. "It looks like a piece of modern art."

"Some people do hang them on their walls like pictures." Uncle Rackham pointed to a twirly-shaped shell. "That's my island there."

The sticks made a pattern on either side of the island.

"Those two sticks show where the strongest currents flow," Uncle Rackham explained. "My island is right in the middle. It can get quite scary where the two currents meet, as you'll see in a moment."

Uncle Rackham pointed ahead. The sea rose up and seemed to form a hill, but it wasn't a wave. The water didn't move – it just stayed there, defying gravity.

"Batten down the hatches!" Caw Caw squawked.

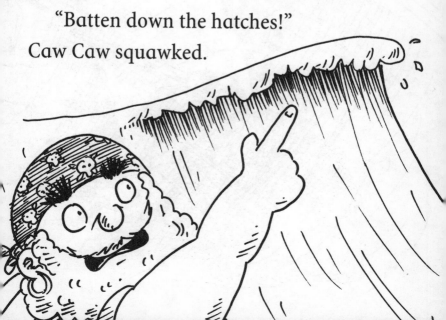

"Hold on tight!" Uncle Rackham turned the boat to face the mountain of water and sailed directly towards it. The little boat climbed higher and higher. Axel felt the current dragging them sideways, faster and faster.

The noise was deafening at the top. The sea almost tore itself apart as they bumped over the furious, boiling turmoil of waves and spray.

The boat lurched as the current on the other side pulled them hard in opposite directions.

"Wooooah!" Axel yelled.

And there, on the other side, in still, calm waters, lay Uncle Rackham's perfect little island...well, nearly perfect.

CHAPTER THREE

Axel jumped from the boat and helped his uncle pull it out of the water. He looked puzzled. "What are all these holes on the beach?" he asked.

"That's where I've been diggin' for treasure!" Uncle Rackham roared. There was a wild glint in his eye.

"But there are hundreds of holes,"
Axel said. "It looks like swiss cheese!"

"Arrr! I've been doin' a lot of diggin',"
Uncle Rackham said gruffly. "And
you're going to help me dig a few more
holes, what with you being young and
fit and strong an' all. We'll find that
treasure yet, me lad!"

"You mean you want me to dig lots of holes on my summer holiday?" Axel complained. "Are you sure there's treasure buried here? Have you got a map?"

"Well…of course I have." Uncle Rackham hesitated. "It's…it's just that the treasure doesn't seem to be where the map says it should be. I'll show you."

They walked across the sand to
Uncle Rackham's beach hut. It was
mostly made from coconut leaves and
smelt of fish.

Uncle Rackham pulled an old
piece of parchment from his sea chest
and spread it out. The chest was his
only table.

"*Home, sweet home,*" Caw Caw sang,
as she settled onto her perch.

"Look," Uncle Rackham pointed to a red smudge on the map. "X marks the spot!"

The parchment looked very old. "I found the map hidden in a book," Uncle Rackham explained. "The book tells how Captain Blackheart's pirate ship, the *Golden Goose*, was torn apart by tidal currents. The ship ran aground on this beach and that's where he buried the treasure."

He pointed to the hundreds of holes on the beach. "Mind you, the story also says that Captain Blackheart put a curse on the treasure, so that no one could find it again," Uncle Rackham said. "Maybe the curse is true..." he added sadly.

Axel studied the map. "Are you sure the map is right?" he asked. "Let's take a better look."

They climbed to the top of the only
hill and studied the shape of the island.

"Strange…" Axel muttered. "The
island looks just like the map. It's
shaped like a catherine wheel. It's
almost as if the island is being spun
around by the currents."

Strange lines and marks crisscrossed
the map. The more Axel stared at
them, the more he realised there was
something familiar about them.

Uncle Rackham scratched his stubbly chin.

"The map faces north, so the X *must* be on that beach," he said firmly.

"But how do you know it's north?" Axel asked. "There isn't a compass on the map."

Uncle Rackham humphed and looked confused.

Axel slowly turned the map around.
Then, as if he'd been struck by lightning,
he jumped up, slapped his forehead and
ran down the hill. "I've got an idea!"
he yelled.

By the time Uncle Rackham had
caught up with him, a huge grin covered
Axel's face. Axel placed the stick map
next to the treasure map.

"It's not a curse at all! The currents have spun the beach around the island ever since the treasure was buried," he laughed. "The marks on the map are the same as the stick map. Turn the map sideways and the sticks and the seashells line up! We should be digging over there!"

Axel pointed to a bay that was formed by one of the sandy beaches.

The water was calm there, unlike where the racing current tore past the outside arm of the beach.

"Your treasure is under the water!" Axel announced proudly.

"Oh, bother!" Uncle Rackham grumbled. "I can't swim!"

CHAPTER FOUR

Soon Axel had put his diving equipment on and Uncle Rackham's boat was floating in the bay above where he thought the treasure of the *Golden Goose* had been buried.

"I've been wanting to go scuba diving all summer," Axel said.

"Good thing too," said Uncle Rackham. "I knew you could help!"

Uncle Rackham handed Axel a rope. "Tie this around your waist," he said. "If you get into trouble, tug the rope hard and I'll pull you up faster than you can say, *shiver me timbers!*"

Caw Caw peered into the water and sang, "*Fifteen men on a dead man's chest. Yo, ho, ho! And a bottle of rum!*"

Axel checked his gear and slipped overboard. In the underwater silence, he was all alone with the gurgling sound of his breathing equipment.

The water was crystal clear. Brightly coloured fish swam among the corals that covered the sandy floor. Axel surprised a giant octopus. It waved its tentacles at him before shooting off to find another hiding place.

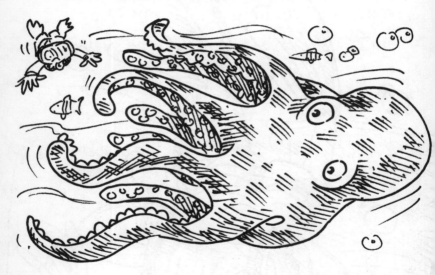

The underwater world was beautiful and exciting. This was what a summer holiday should be like!

Axel dug around in the fine, yellow sand. *Nothing.* How were they ever going to find buried treasure like this?

Then, his fingertips felt something hard. He scooped away the sand and pulled free an old, broken piece of wood. Axel could just make out some letters that were carved into the surface: G...O...O...S...E...

Goose! Axel thought. *The Golden Goose!* Axel felt his heart race. He'd found the wreck of the ship – or a part of it, at least.

Axel looked all around him. The pattern of the corals on the seabed formed a shape – the outline of a sunken ship!

The seabed dropped away as Axel swam the length of the wreck. He was getting much deeper. Where should he start digging?

Suddenly, Axel realised that he was being moved along by a current.

The lovely warm water he'd been swimming in turned icy cold. He felt himself being drawn out to sea. He would never survive if he became tangled up in the raging tidal currents that swept around the island!

He turned to swim back to the shallower water.

Then he stopped in shock. Five or six enormous sharks were barring his way. They swam lazily between him and the safe, still water. They rolled their wicked eyes and watched him with great interest, as if they were looking at their dinner.

Axel felt his breathing speed up.

Don't panic! he told himself.
He pulled hard on his rope and
immediately felt himself being pulled to
the surface. One of the sharks made its
move and swam towards him.

As Uncle Rackham hauled Axel onto the boat, the shark's head broke the surface. Its eyes rolled madly in their sockets. Its gaping mouth opened wide. Time stood still for a moment. Axel was so close he could have counted every one of the vicious, razor-sharp teeth.

"Sharks!" Axel gasped.

CHAPTER FIVE

The boat had drifted quite close to the raging current. Axel heard the sound of the turbulent water where the two currents collided. But he could hear something else too – the whine of…an outboard motor!

A boat appeared from nowhere. It flew through the air as it was tossed over the hill of foaming water. The sun reflected on a camera lens.

Axel's heart sank. "It's Archie Flash from *Celebrity Gossip Magazine*. He's found us!"

"Caw!" screamed Caw Caw and flew into the air.

Archie was too busy taking pictures. His speedboat roared past them, missing them by millimetres. Uncle Rackham's boat was tossed about in its wake.

Axel grabbed for a rope to hang on to. But he missed, wobbled, lost his balance and felt himself tumbling over the side of the boat.

The cold water grabbed him with icy fingers and began drawing him down and down. The current was too strong. He managed to put on his mouthpiece – now at least he could breathe. But how much air was left in the tank?

The current sucked him down faster and faster, dragging him along the seabed, out towards the open, raging ocean!

Axel scrabbled for something to hold on to. He dug his hands into the sand, desperate to find anything solid.

And then he felt something deep in the sand. His fingers curled round it and held on tight. It was enough to anchor his position.

What is it? It feels like…

Axel forgot the danger – his treasure-hunting instinct took over. He scraped the sand away with his other hand. Excitement shot through him as he caught a glimpse of something yellow and shiny.

Gold coins and silvery pearls spilled onto the sand! As Axel reached out to grab them, the rope tightened around his waist and he felt himself being hauled upwards to safety.

Axel's arm broke the surface first. His hand gripped the stem of a golden chalice. It was encrusted with rubies, sapphires and diamonds. His fingers had refused to let go of it.

"Look what I found!" he yelled, pulling his mouthpiece out and gulping down lungfuls of fresh air. "Pirate treasure!"

"*Pieces of eight! Pieces of eight!*"
Caw Caw shrieked excitedly.

"Smile for the camera!" Archie
Flash called from his boat. His camera
whirred as he took shot after shot.
Archie knew that this was a really
great story!

CHAPTER SIX

"I don't believe it!" said Mum.

They were back home in their huge city apartment. The butler had bought all the newspapers and magazines for them.

"We go for a quiet holiday to get away from it all, and Axel ends up in the papers!"

The picture of Axel holding the chalice above his head was on every front page. The magazines featured long articles with photographs of all the treasure he and Uncle Rackham had discovered.

"It was so dangerous!" said Dad. "You could have been eaten by sharks!"

"And what about Captain Blackheart's curse?" Mum gasped.

Axel smiled. "Oh, we lured the sharks out into the current with lumps of meat and never saw them again. As for Captain Blackheart's curse – well… pirates curse just about everything, don't they?"

CELEBRITY GOSSIP MAGAZINE

AXEL STORM DISCOVERS PIRATE TREASURE

Fearless Axel Storm turned his holidays into an adventure this summer. Braving Captain Blackheart's curse, sharks and a giant octopus, he discovered a million-pound fortune of underwater pirate treasure.

"Axel's treasure is of international historic importance," said Henry Forsythe at the History Museum.

Axel said,

"I WAS REALLY BORED ON HOLIDAY AND THIS GAVE ME SOMETHING TO DO."

Axel's Uncle Rackham said, "That boy can really swim!"

His parrot, Caw Caw, said, "*No comment!*"

By ace reporter, Archie Flash.

SHOO RAYNER

ALL PRICED AT £8.99

Orchard Books are available from all good bookshops,
or can be ordered from our website: www.orchardbooks.co.uk,
or telephone 01235 827702, or fax 01235 827703.